THIS WALKER BOOK BELONGS TO:

_____

_____

_____

_____

In Memory of
Humpty Dumpty

First published 1994 by Walker Books Ltd
87 Vauxhall Walk, London SE11 5HJ

© 1994 Miko Imai

8 10 12 14 15 13 11 9 7

This book has been typeset in Stone Informal.

Printed in Hong Kong/China

British Library Cataloguing in Publication Data
A catalogue record for this book is available
from the British Library.

ISBN 0-7445-3605-7

LITTLE LUMPTY

Miko Imai

WALKER BOOKS
AND SUBSIDIARIES
LONDON • BOSTON • SYDNEY

In the little town of Dumpty there was a high wall.
Humpty Dumpty had fallen from it long, long ago.
But people still remembered him.

Every day children played by the wall and sang,
"Humpty Dumpty sat on the wall.
Humpty Dumpty had a great fall."

Little Lumpty loved the wall and always
dreamed about climbing to the top.

"Don't ever do that," Lumpty's mother said.
"Remember, all the king's horses and all the king's men
couldn't put Humpty Dumpty together again."

But Little Lumpty couldn't stop thinking about the wall.

One day, on his way home from school, he
found a long ladder and dragged it to the wall.

He climbed up …
and up … and up.

At last he reached the top. "Oh, there's my house!

And there's my school! I can almost touch the clouds!"

Lumpty was so happy that he danced along like a tightrope walker.

"If only my friends could see me now!"

But then Little Lumpty looked down. IT WAS A BIG

MISTAKE. His legs began to shake and tremble.

"Oh, no! I don't think I can get back to the ladder."

"What if I'm not home by dinner time?"

It was getting dark and the birds were flying home
to their nests, but still Little Lumpty could not move.
Suddenly he remembered Humpty Dumpty's great fall.

"Help! Help!" screamed Little Lumpty.

Everyone in town rushed out to see what was wrong.

"How can we save him?" asked an old man.
"We need a big blanket!" said Lumpty's mother,
and she ran home to get one.

They stretched it out at the bottom of the wall.
"Jump, Lumpty, jump!
  Jump, Lumpty, jump!"

Little Lumpty took a deep breath and
threw himself into the dark night air.

He bounced once,

twice,

three times,

and then came safely to rest on the blanket.

"Mummy, I'm sorry," he said. "I just had to see what it would be like on top."

Little Lumpty was so glad to be home.

"But I still love that wall,"
he whispered to the moon,
just before he fell asleep.

MORE WALKER PAPERBACKS
For You to Enjoy

SEBASTIAN'S TRUMPET
by Miko Imai

The three bear triplets each get a special present on their birthday:
Theodore gets a drum; Oswald gets a banjo and Sebastian gets a trumpet –
but try as he might, he just can't get it to play. Will his birthday end in tears?

"An excellent picture book…
Miko Imai's expressive illustrations will charm both parents and toddlers."
The School Librarian

0-7445-4395-9   £4.99

THE GRUMPALUMP
by Sarah Hayes/Barbara Firth

Just what is the grumpalump? A mole can roll on it, a dove can shove it, a yak can whack it
and an armadillo can use it for a pillow. But what is it, and why is it so grumpy?

"Jauntily drawn and painted… Irresistible, easy-to-read fantasy." *The Observer*

0-7445-2021-5   £5.99

WUZZY TAKES OFF
by Robin and Helen Lester/Miko Imai

In this story featuring a classic Gund soft toy, Wuzzy, the woodland bear,
longs for a great adventure – and what greater adventure could there be than going to the moon!
But Wuzzy's moon looks oddly familiar…

0-7445-5226-5   £3.99

Walker Paperbacks are available from most booksellers, or by post from B.B.C.S., P.O. Box 941, Hull, North Humberside HU1 3YQ
24 hour telephone credit card line 01482 224626

To order, send: Title, author, ISBN number and price for each book ordered, your full name and address,
cheque or postal order payable to BBCS for the total amount and allow the following for postage and packing:
UK and BFPO: £1.00 for the first book, and 50p for each additional book to a maximum of £3.50.
Overseas and Eire: £2.00 for the first book, £1.00 for the second and 50p for each additional book.

Prices and availability are subject to change without notice.